Lesson Plans

PRAISE FOR *STORYSHARES*

"One of the brightest innovators and game-changers in the education industry."
– Forbes

"Your success in applying research-validated practices to promote literacy serves as a valuable model for other organizations seeking to create evidence-based literacy programs."
- Library of Congress

"We need powerful social and educational innovation, and Storyshares is breaking new ground. The organization addresses critical problems facing our students and teachers. I am excited about the strategies it brings to the collective work of making sure every student has an equal chance in life."
– Teach For America

"Around the world, this is one of the up-and-coming trailblazers changing the landscape of literacy and education."
- International Literacy Association

"It's the perfect idea. There's really nothing like this. I mean wow, this will be a wonderful experience for young people."   - Andrea Davis Pinkney, Executive Director, Scholastic

"Reading for meaning opens opportunities for a lifetime of learning. Providing emerging readers with engaging texts that are designed to offer both challenges and support for each individual will improve their lives for years to come. Storyshares is a wonderful start."
- David Rose, Co-founder of CAST & UDL

Lesson Plans

Joanna Szeto

STORYSHARES

Story Share, Inc.
New York. Boston. Philadelphia.

Published in the United States by Story Share, Inc.

The characters and events in this book are fictitious. Any similarity to real persons, living or dead, is entirely coincidental.

Storyshares
Story Share, Inc.
24 N. Bryn Mawr Avenue #340
Bryn Mawr, PA 19010-3304
www.storyshares.org

Inspiring reading with a new kind of book.

Interest Level: Middle School
Grade Level Equivalent: 3.1

9798885979764

Book design by Storyshares

Printed in the United States of America

Storyshares Presents

1

It started after my parents got me a new computer on my birthday.

At first, I used it for homework and research. Then I discovered the games on the internet.

I was addicted.

I turned in more and more incomplete assignments. Then Ms. Wu asked to see my mother.

She gave me a letter for my mom. I lost it in the mess in my desk. But since my mom is a teacher, they ran into each other at a professional development event.

I was busted.

I thought my mom would yell at the dinner table. I was positive she would scream and shout.

Instead, she calmly asked, "Dylan, what are you going to do about your homework?"

I stopped eating, with my fork halfway to my mouth.

Was this a trick question? I wondered. *She was actually asking my opinion?*

"What do you mean he hasn't been doing his homework?" my dad boomed.

He didn't want my grades to slip. He didn't want me to get kicked off the soccer team. He wanted me to be a famous soccer player someday. I might have been, if we were still in China. Here, none of the other kids really care about soccer.

"Just some of it," I admitted. "I'm acing all my tests, though."

My dad breathed a sigh of relief.

"That's great," he said. "I knew my son was smart."

My mom frowned. "What about your teacher?"

Since she's a teacher herself, she hates it when anyone doesn't do their homework. It's an educator thing.

"If you're so worried about it, why don't you do it yourself?" I asked.

I shocked myself with the words coming out of my mouth.

My mom opened her mouth to answer, but nothing came out. Finally, she set down her chopsticks and looked at me.

"Okay," she said. "But with one condition."

"What?" I asked.

It couldn't be good. There was no way she would ever agree to do my homework. And even if she did, there had to be some law against parents doing their kid's homework.

"If I do your homework for a day," she said with a smile, "then you'll have to do my job for a day."

I stared at her. I waited for her to laugh, to tell me she was joking.

She wasn't joking.

"Fine," I agreed. "Fourth grade wasn't that hard. I got straight As last year."

"Then it's a deal," my mom said.

She stuck out her hand for me to shake.

2

The next day, I handed my mom's letter to Ms. Wu. She read it as I played with the zipper on my jacket.

"Okay," she said. "I'll give you the homework assignment for tomorrow."

She copied the assignments from her lesson plan book.

"You're still responsible for tonight's homework, but you can turn it in on Monday," she said.

She smiled a little too much as she handed me my homework.

I barely listened to the lesson. I wondered what trick they had planned against me. Surely, teaching a bunch of fourth graders couldn't be worse than the hours of homework I had each night.

When my mom picked me up after school, she made me sit in the back seat.

"What's all that stuff in the front?" I asked.

"It's everything you will need for tomorrow," she said.

She looked at me in the rearview mirror. I smiled back weakly.

In the garage, I handed my mom the homework. Two grammar worksheets, two pages of math, and an hour of reading for the reading log.

My mom put a pile of teacher's manuals into my arms. There were four for reading, one for math, and another for science. On the very top, she put her lesson plan book.

"If you need any help, just let me know," she said.

"Uh-huh," I grunted.

Somehow, the piles didn't seem equal.

After dinner, I opened up the lesson plan book on my bed. It looked like a long day.

Pick up the students from the yard, take attendance, and collect homework.

Reading groups, recess, P.E., math, lunch. DEAR time, read aloud, science, phonics, homework, and dismissal.

The second page showed the reading group schedule. It had a rotation every twenty minutes. One group had computers. Another small group worked with a paraprofessional. One group worked independently on journaling.

So that was it. I grabbed the sheet of paper. I ran down the stairs and shoved it in front of my mom's face.

She was reading a novel for the reading log.

"You expect me to do small groups?" I asked.

"No, that is my schedule," Mom said, smiling. "There's another schedule for substitutes in the side pocket."

I raced back upstairs to find my new schedule.

It looked exactly the same, except the reading groups had been replaced by whole class writing. We would read a book like *The Very Hungry Caterpillar.* Then the class would write their own stories based on the model.

It was easy, except for the boring book.

I ran over to the bookshelf. I pulled out *Alexander and the Terrible, Horrible, No Good, Very Bad Day.* This would be much better than a toddler book. I crossed out my mom's book and wrote in mine.

Then I went through each subject. I checked to make sure I knew what I would have to teach.

We could play War Ball for P.E.

Fractions and the solar system weren't very hard. I could deal with them. I'd gotten straight As in all my classes last year.

Lesson planning had only taken a half hour. There was still plenty of time before dinner.

I ran downstairs to watch television.

Mom was still cuddled up on the couch, reading.

"No television until everyone's finished with homework," she said.

I shrugged and went back upstairs. I didn't mind the tradeoff.

3

Mom made me wear a suit and tie for my big day as a teacher. No big deal. I figured it would be easier to get respect if I didn't look like I belonged in the class.

The principal must have been in on it. He announced to the entire school that I, Mr. Jin, would be the fourth-grade substitute for the day.

Taking attendance was hard. I couldn't pronounce their names. They need to get English names.

Collecting homework wasn't any better. Four rows of eight students. But I didn't have enough homework from each row, even with the empty chairs.

"Who's missing homework?" I asked. "Raise your hand if you didn't do it."

I wrote down the names of the students who didn't turn in an assignment.

"If you want to learn English, you'd better do your homework," I said in English, and then again in Chinese.

Was this the point my mom was trying to make? I wondered.

Except I already know English. I don't need to do my homework to get a good grade.

Twenty-eight students stared back at me. I didn't have much time to think about my own problems.

"Story time," I said.

Half the students turned to face me. The other half went on with whatever they were doing.

"Eyes on me," I said.

I couldn't believe that came out of my mouth. I sounded like a kindergarten teacher.

I couldn't tell if they understood me, or if it was the tone of my voice. I didn't care. I had their attention.

I opened up the book and began reading.

Immediately a hand shot up.

"Yes?" I asked.

"Can you tell it in Chinese?" a girl with pigtails asked.

"If I tell it in Chinese, you won't be able to learn English," I explained.

Still, I tried to act out as much as I could. *The Very Hungry Caterpillar* started to seem like a good idea. Too bad I had left it under my bed.

I knew they wouldn't be able to write their own stories based on the book I chose. So instead, we wrote one together about a character named Kaiqi.

"It will be called *Kaiqi and the Horrible, Awful, Dreadful, Very Terrible Day,*" I said.

The students laughed. I was glad I had their attention.

"What do you think happened to Kaiqi when she woke up this morning?" I asked.

One or two students raised their hands.

"You can say it in Chinese if you want," I added.

More students raised their hands. I called on six students.

"How about this: Kaiqi left a partly eaten chocolate bar in the pocket of her pajamas. She woke up with chocolate and ants all over her!" one student said.

With each addition to the story, I called on five or six hands. Then I added one of their ideas to the story. By the end of the story, our main character, Kaiqi, sure was having a terrible day.

"Let's read the entire story together," I said.

I pointed to the words as I read the story out loud. The students who could read followed along. Then I passed out lined paper.

"Now, you will write your own story," I said. "Use your own name in the title. You can use different synonyms for the word 'bad' in your title. You can also copy the story from the board, but remember to change it to your own name."

That was way too easy. But then one boy, Weixu, raised his hand.

"How do I write *'lor see?'*" he asked.

"Huh? Screwdriver?" I asked. "Can you give me the whole sentence?"

"Oy tou eng yu zhek lor see," he said.

It sounded like something from another planet.

"Anyone know what he's saying?" I asked. I looked around the room.

"He's speaking Taishanese," said another student. "He wants to write '*Ngoh tau deng yau dzek lo sue*.'"

I laughed and wrote, "There's a mouse on my head" on the board.

4

Recess was fun.

I joined them in a game of four square. Just when I got to be King, an argument between two third graders pulled me away.

"You hit it out of bounds," one of them said.

"No, I hit it on the line," the other said.

"It was out," the first student argued.

"No, it wasn't," the other said.

"You can just have a replay," I explained.

"But that's not fair," they both complained.

I spent the rest of recess trying to prevent a fight. Still, I would have let them play for the rest of the morning. But Ms. Ng showed up with her class.

She gave me a thumbs-up as my students lined up to go back to class.

Math was a nightmare.

I read the answers to last night's homework. One of the students insisted that I was wrong.

"I can't be wrong," I said. "I got it from the teacher's manual."

The student, Queenie, wouldn't give up.

"My father helped me with that problem. He says the answer is three and one half," she said.

"Okay, okay," I said. "Show me on the board."

She carefully wrote five and one third minus one and five sixths on the board. Imagine my surprise when I found out that the teacher's manual had the wrong answer.

My face was still red when I explained the reason for the wrong answer.

What's the point of having a teacher's manual when it's wrong? I wondered.

Then I found out some students didn't understand fractions.

"You can't add the numerators and the denominators," I explained to Dehao for the fifth time.

He was fine when I stood next to him. But by the time I'd circled the class, his answers made no sense.

"Didn't you learn this last year?" I asked.

"I was in second grade last year," Dehao whispered.

"Why did you skip third grade?" I asked.

It definitely wasn't because of his math skills.

"Because I'm ten years old," Dehao said.

I must have looked confused.

"They assign us by age," Queenie explained.

Before I could come up with an answer, the lunch bell rang.

Peanut butter and jelly wouldn't be enough to get through the rest of the day. I felt like the kids had sucked me dry of all my energy.

I walked into the teachers' lunchroom with my Superman lunchbox.

The teachers looked up and smiled.

"How was your day?" asked Ms. Ng, the second-grade teacher.

"I haven't heard a lot of yelling yet," said Mrs. Fong, the teacher across the hall.

"Yelling?" I asked.

"Your mom yells a lot," Mrs. Fong said. "Luckily, her two big headaches are absent today."

I smiled weakly.

5

I didn't read much during DEAR time. Instead, I patrolled the room like a police officer.

They talked more than they read.

Students who *were* reading flipped through their books faster than a movie. I had to ban students from changing books within the fifteen-minute time limit.

Soon, I was getting better at choosing books. I read *The True Story of the Three Little Pigs* after students retold the original story in Chinese.

I felt like I was ready for anything by the time science came along.

"Let's see if everyone remembers the nine planets," I said.

"Ms. Liu said there's only eight," Queenie said.

"Yes, last year one of them got demoted," I said. "Do you know which one?"

"*Ming Wong Sing,*" she said.

I had no idea if that translation was right or wrong.

"The answer is Pluto," I said.

"What will happen if our sun blows up?" Dehao asked.

"I don't know," I said slowly. "But it probably won't happen until you're already dead."

"What about the leaking oil in the Gulf of Mexico?" Weixu asked. "Will it affect us now?"

"That's a good question," I said, just as slowly.

It still didn't give me enough time to think of an answer, though.

"Have you thought about what you are going to do to make the world better?" Queenie asked.

Too many questions, and I didn't have the answer to any of them.

"How about I tell you a little secret," I said. "I'm only in fifth grade. I don't have all the answers."

"We already knew that," Queenie said.

"You did?" I asked.

"Ms. Liu told us you were coming," Queenie said. "She said you would teach us a lot of things."

"Ms. Liu said you didn't like to do homework," Dehao said. "But you could help us find the answers to a lot of our questions."

I thought about that for a while.

"We *could* learn the effects of the oil in the Gulf of Mexico by doing a little research," I said. "Does everyone know how to search the internet?"

A few students nodded.

"We also need to know how oil affects the environment," I said. "My mom should have a huge section about the environment in the classroom library."

"I'll find them," Dehao said.

The rest of the science lesson disappeared into chaos as students broke off into groups. Each group researched their assigned tasks.

Dismissal didn't happen until fifteen minutes after the bell rang. The after-school teacher and five parents waited patiently outside while I talked about the homework.

* * *

That weekend, I finished all of my own homework by Saturday morning. But I was still working hard on the computer all the way into Monday.

I chatted with some of the students in my mom's fourth-grade newcomer class. I had to use my old Chinese-English dictionary to figure out what some of them were saying and asking. I helped them with their projects and with their research.

After that, I even surprised myself with a little research of my own.

"How to become a teacher..." I typed.

About The Author

Joanna Szeto was born in Hong Kong, but lives in San Francisco. She is married with two kids and works as a Chinese bilingual elementary school teacher. She loves including her students and kids in her stories. She writes stories in English and Chinese. She writes and illustrates her little Chinese readers to sell on her store, Working Wonders, at teacherspayteachers.com. She has four Chinese books published on ichinesereader.com. Her story "Lesson Plans" is published on storyshares.org. When she's not writing she enjoys watching Chinese dramas, reading, painting, sewing, or having fun with her kids.

About The Publisher

Story Shares is a nonprofit focused on supporting the millions of teens and adults who struggle with reading by creating a new shelf in the library specifically for them. The ever-growing collection features content that is compelling and culturally relevant for teens and adults, yet still readable at a range of lower reading levels.

Story Shares generates content by engaging deeply with writers, bringing together a community to create this new kind of book. With more intriguing and approachable stories to choose from, the teens and adults who have fallen behind are improving their skills and beginning to discover the joy of reading. For more information, visit storyshares.org.

Easy to Read. Hard to Put Down.